I Love You Too, I Love You Three

Written by **Wendy Tugwood**
Illustrations by **Sheila McGraw**

FIREFLY BOOKS

A Firefly Book

Published by Firefly Books Ltd. 2016
Copyright © 2016 Firefly Books Ltd.
Text copyright © 2016 Wendy Tugwood
Illustrations copyright © 2016 Sheila McGraw

First printing

Publisher Cataloging-in-Publication Data (U.S.)
Names: Tugwood, Wendy, author.
Title: I love you too, I love you three / Wendy Tugwood.
Description: Richmond Hill, Ontario, Canada : Firefly Books, 2016. | Summary: "As every parent knows, there is nothing more stressful than being away from a child even if it's only for a few days. In this heartwarming book, the author captures perfectly how the love between a mother and child helps cope with separation" – Provided by publisher.
Identifiers: ISBN 978-1-77085-784-1 (hardcover)
Subjects: LCSH: Mother and child—Juvenile fiction. | Separation anxiety – Juvenile fiction.
Classification: LCC PZ7.1T849Ilo |DDC [Fic] – dc23

Library and Archives Canada Cataloguing in Publication
Tugwood, Wendy, 1967-, author
I love you too, I love you three / Wendy Tugwood.
ISBN 978-1-77085-784-1 (hardback)
I. Title.
PZ7.1.T85Il 2016   j813'.6   C2016-901550-5

Published in the United States by
Firefly Books (U.S.) Inc.
P.O. Box 1338, Ellicott Station
Buffalo, New York 14205

Published in Canada by
Firefly Books Ltd.
50 Staples Avenue, Unit 1
Richmond Hill, Ontario L4B 0A7

Printed in China

The publisher gratefully acknowledges the financial support for our publishing program by the Government of Canada through the Canada Book Fund as administered by the Department of Canadian Heritage.

Dedication

This book is dedicated to my three beautiful children:
Michael, Gabriel, and Rebecca. I love you three!

Wendy Tugwood

For Max, Graham, and James...
I love you three.

Sheila McGraw

When we're apart I miss you so,
    I wish I didn't have to go.

I miss your face, your touch, your smell,
    Your silliness I know so well.

I think of how you sing to me,
   "I love you too … I love you three!"

On goes our love and counting game,
   A game that always ends the same.

When it's time again for slumber,
I'll be there to count our numbers.

"I love you one,
I love you two."

And now I say goodnight to you.

"I love you three,
   I love you four."

I move and stand beside the door.

"I love you five,
    I love you six."

I turn and blow a gentle kiss.

"I love you seven,
    I love you eight."

And now it's really getting late.

"I love you nine,
I love you ten."

Go back and start at one, again.

And though I have to go awhile,
I'll be home soon, my darling child,

To tuck you safe into your bed,
My precious one, my sleepyhead.

When darkness all around you falls,
    And crickets sound their mating calls,

As moonlight gently fills your room,
Your dreams begin to sprout, then bloom.

I start us off with "I love you."

Then you reply "I love you too."

And when you are away from me,
Remember this, "I love you three!"